D1203096

Gladly

Rachelle Ginee
author

Anna Abramskaya
illustrator

For Alex...may you always find happiness.

Gladly the llama
Had always felt down.
He had sad droopy ears
And a big llama frown.

His meadow was merry
With a sunny blue sky,
But poor Gladly would sit
And just snuffle and cry.

He would splash in his stream
Full of fun, floaty bubbles,
Though it still didn't help
To fix his sad troubles.

But this day was special –
You might call it strange –
As this was the day
He wanted to change.

"I want to be happy,
And make this my vow –
I'll start an adventure
To figure out how."

So he took some bananas,
His toothbrush and fiddle,
And set off with his pack
Tied on tight to his middle.

He marched up the trail.
He travelled for hours.
And then a small bird
Burst out of the flowers.

Hummmmm...

She was green on her chest
With a fluffy pink tummy.
She cheeped down to Gladly,
"Hi! My name is Hummey!"

She flew down to him,
Landing right on his head!
"You sure do look sad,"
Ms. Hummey Bird said.

"I want to be happy,
And I've made this my quest.
I've set out to find
What might help me best."

Eager to help,
Hummey shared with the llama
Some ancient bird-knowledge
Passed down from her mama...

"Joy comes from a place
That lives inside you.
Just think happy thoughts –
It's so easy to do!

Start with some words,
Some words that you say,
Declare, I am grateful,
I am grateful today!

If in your heart
You feel sadness or fear,
Just blast it away
With good thoughts and cheer."

So Gladly thought hard,
"What am I grateful for?"
And for every one thought
He came up with ten more!

He thought of his home
With the beautiful trees
And the sweet daisy flowers
In the warm summer breeze.

This helped Gladly realize
That when he'd been sad,
His thoughts were caught up
With things that seemed bad.

"Well, now that I focus
On all that is great,
I can feel a big shift
In my happiness state!"

He clip-clopped along
Pressing on with his travel.
With this happiness quest
He had more to unravel.

He trekked and he trudged
Till he saw a small lake.
It looked perfectly splendid
For a quick llama break.

He peered at the water
And out of the muck
Came waddling towards him
A very strange duck.

He said, "My name's Chuckles,"
With giggles and hoots.
He was wearing green goggles
And polka dot boots!

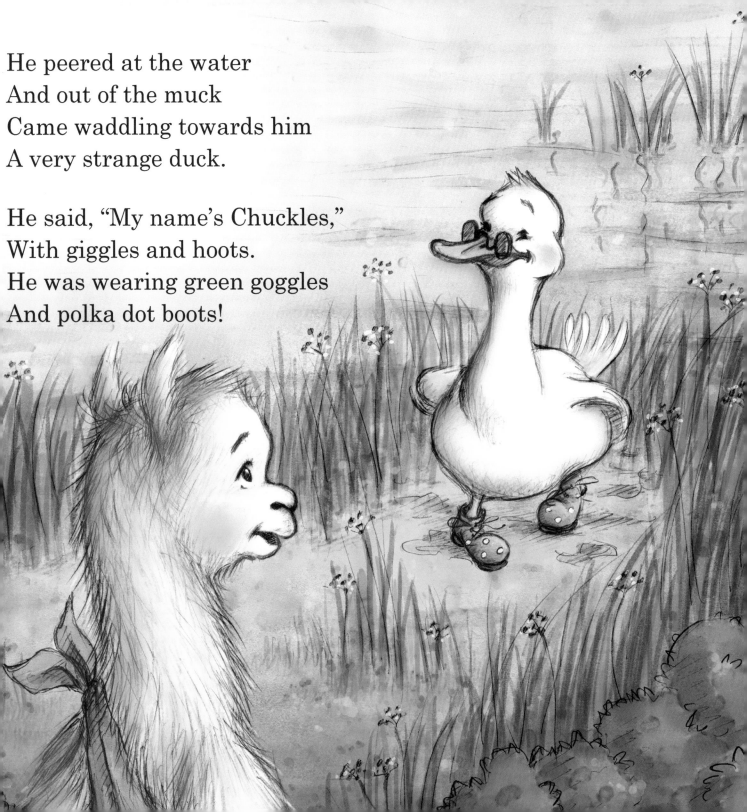

Said Chuckles to Gladly,
"Don't go in a hurry!
We're friendly, I promise,
So no need to worry.

You have come to Lake Fun,
Place of laughter and play.
We make room for joy
In our lives everyday.

Sometimes we're grumpy
And sad, this is true,
But we squash these with fun –
We can show you how too!"

He gave a big grin
And another long giggle,
A song started then
And he danced with a wiggle.

Then out from the brush
What next did appear?
A bright blue banjo,
Strummed by Bucky the Deer.

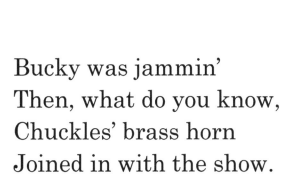

Bucky was jammin'
Then, what do you know,
Chuckles' brass horn
Joined in with the show.

Soon Gladly found out
He was caught in the middle.
So he figured, "Why not?"
And bust out his fiddle.

From another direction,
With a swirl and a swoop,
Came a goose named Miranda
With a pink hula-hoop.

Gladly twirled and he danced
And he played on his fiddle.
The party was helping
To solve his sad riddle.

How easy it was
Just to stop being sad
If you focused your life
On the fun to be had!

So as he moved on
Down the trail from the lake,
He said, "Thank you, my friends,
Your lesson I'll take."

Further on down the road
Came some noise from the trees.
It was buzzing and singing
From some bumbly bees.

Soon he was surrounded,
There were bees by the dozen.
He met Beatrice and Buzzie
And Bumbles, their cousin.

One piece of advice
Buzzle offered to lend...
"It's very important
To give to a friend.

Bees help one another,
We give and we share.
So come watch our team,
Our hive is right there!"

Gloopy globs of gold honey
Dripped down from the tree.
It was all made with love,
Like a gift from each bee.

As eight bees made honey,
Three bees helped the Queen,
Twelve bees scouted pollen –
What a fabulous scene!

He noticed how Buzzle
Helped Bumbles with care,
And Beeatrice gave pollen
For the flowers to share.

Watching them give
Made Gladly feel good,
So he wanted to share
His own gift, if he could.

He said to the bees,
"Well I recently grew
this new happy smile.
Can I share it with you?"

And right where the frown
Used to be on his face,
A shiny new grin
Spread joy in its place.

And as his grin grew
For his new friends to share,
Joy spread through the llama
From his toes to his hair.

Gladly learned then
That for happiness living,
The last missing piece
Was the true joy of giving.

He felt that his quest
Was now fully complete,
So he headed for home
While skipping his feet.

As Gladly reached home.
He held his head high.
"I can do anything,
Just as long as I try!

I'm so happy now,
And I'm feeling so glad,
But I do miss my friends
And the fun that we've had."

Just then from a tree
Down Ms. Hummey Bird flew,
and as Gladly saw her
His grin grew and grew.

He saw Bucky Deer
With his banjo in hand,
Then up waddled Chuckles –
They brought the whole band!

Miranda came in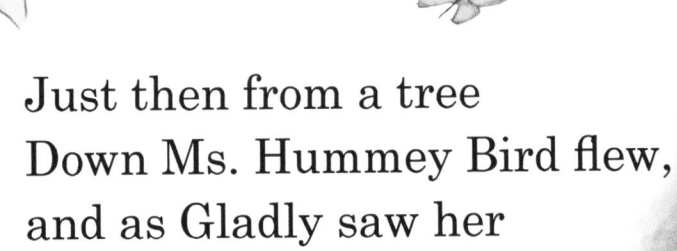
With her hoop in a swirl.
She spun it around
With a twist and a twirl!

The bees swarmed in next,
Buzzing loud with great cheer,
And Gladly cried out,
"I'm thrilled you're all here!"

Gladly's heart became full
and the love was so yummy,
It felt like warm hugs
dancing round in his tummy.

So that's how it happened.
He was no longer sad.
Every day would be happy.
Gladly was glad!

Copyright © 2017 by Bee Positive Publishing
All rights reserved. This book or any portion thereof
may not be reproduced or used in any manner whatsoever
without the express written permission of the publisher
except for the use of brief quotations in a book review.
Printed in the United States of America
First Printing, 2017
ISBN 978-0-9997185-7-5
Bee Positive Publishing
Graeagle, CA 96103
www.beepositivepublishing.com

The End

CPSIA information can be obtained at www.ICGtesting.com
Printed in the USA
LVIW01n1521110118
562710LV00014B/289